The Great Bike Race

THE GREAT BIKE RACE

by

Kathy Stinson

For Alexandra —
Ride on!

Kathy

April 2012

James Lorimer & Company Ltd., Publishers
Toronto

James Lorimer & Company Ltd. acknowledges the support of the Ontario Arts Council. We acknowledge the support of the Government of Canada through the Book Publishing Industry Development Program (BPIDP) for our publishing activities. We acknowledge the support of the Canada Council for the Arts for our publishing program. We acknowledge the support of the Government of Ontario through the Ontario Media Development Corporation's Ontario Book Initiative.

Cover design: Iris Glaser

The Canada Council | Le Conseil des Arts
for the Arts | du Canada

ONTARIO ARTS COUNCIL
CONSEIL DES ARTS DE L'ONTARIO

Library and Archives Canada Cataloguing in Publication

Stinson, Kathy
[Great Pebble Creek bike race]
    The great bike race / Kathy Stinson.

(Streetlights)
First published under title: The great Pebble Creek bike race .
ISBN-13: 978-1-55028-890-2   ISBN-10: 1-55028-890-3

    I. Title. II. Series.
PS8587.T56G7 2005   jC813'.54   C2005-904862-X

James Lorimer & Company Ltd.,
Publishers
317 Adelaide Street West
Suite 1002
Toronto, Ontario, M5V 1P9
www.lorimer.ca
Printed and bound in Canada.

Distributed in the
United States by:
Orca Book Publishers
P.O. Box 468
Custer, WA USA
98240-0468

THANKS TO MY editor, Hadley Dyer, for her enthusiasm for this project, for her guidance, and her friendship.

Special thanks to Linda Wall and Brenda Kristensen for the time they invested in helping me to understand Amanda's world and language. For their interest, thanks also to Clifton Carbin, Ron Foster, Robyn Sandford, and Diane Magee.

To Peter for the mystery and adventure he brings to my summers

1

"NOT AGAIN," MATT muttered.

He hopped off his bike to reattach the drooping chain. He straightened the crooked seat and pedalled on — past the library, Joe's Deli, and the Viewmore Video store. He stopped to peer into the window of Silver Streak Cycle & Sports.

Straddling his old bike, Matt admired the gleaming new Supercycle Impulse FS-MTB on display. With its eighteen speeds, cantilever brakes, aluminum rims, and knobby tires, it was a beauty — no question. And its price tag was a whopper. He'd be an old man, for sure, before he could save up enough for a bike anywhere near as good as the Impulse. If only he could figure out a way to get his parents to buy him a new bike — *any* new bike. Having a birthday in December was so useless.

Maybe he should try to get his old bike stolen. Then his parents would have to get him a new one. But who'd want to steal a bike with more rust on it than paint, half a handgrip missing, and a loose seat? Matt probably couldn't pay someone to take the old clunker away.

Maybe he should just "lose" it in the ravine or something. *My bike? Oh, I lost it.* Except he could hear what his parents would say about that. *You what? Well, you can hardly expect us to fork over for a new bike when you couldn't take care of the old one.* Besides, his mom had been laid off at work, so there'd be no extra money for a bike for a while.

Matt flicked at the loose chrome curling off his handlebar and made himself ride away from the beautiful bike on display. The afternoon sun beat down hard. Heat rippled off the pavement.

On the front porch of the dark, two-storey

house at the top of Matt's street — the house a lot of the kids in Pebble Creek said was haunted — sat Mr. Grubb. The old man's pale skin made him look almost ghostly. He was taller than anyone else Matt knew, and always looked like he was scowling. As Matt rode by, Mr. Grubb waved his cane.

Matt almost started to speed away — out of habit — but then waved back instead.

From behind him, Matt heard a voice. "Don't you get tired of riding that beat-up old thing?" And on his gleaming, red, hyper-grind freestyle BMX, David whizzed right past.

"No," Matt snarled, "I love it." He rode hard to catch up to his weird new friend. "Why do you brainers always ask the dumbest questions?"

"To keep losers like you on your toes."

Matt shook his head, hot inside his helmet. "You're lousy at baseball, you spend your Saturday mornings at Greek school, your shirt is always tucked in neatly, and you're calling *me* a loser?"

"So, why are you hanging out with me then, if I'm such a loser?"

Matt pretended to think about David's question. "How about because I like your bike and once in a blue moon you let me ride it?"

"Loser," said David.

"Geek," said Matt.

David laughed. "Wanna go for an ice cream?"

Matt wiped sweat and his shaggy brown hair from his forehead. "Good idea" he said.

The only sign of life as Matt and David rode past the small boxy houses on Booth Street was a cat stalking a butterfly. All the other kids on the street were away. Just before the boys got to the ravine, Matt said, "Look," and skidded to a stop. A moving van was parked in front of the house where his old friend Sam used to live. "Someone must be moving in."

David said, "I wonder if they've got any kids."

The movers were just starting to unload the van. A big burly man carried a houseplant and a floor lamp through the open door of the empty house. From the back of the truck his partner lifted a green bike. It had no crossbar.

"Oh, no," groaned Matt. "Not a girl living in Sam's house!" Matt and David rolled their eyes and took off.

Even Matt's old rattletrap of a bicycle whizzed smoothly down the winding ravine path. It was cool under the trees that grew there. At the bottom of the ravine they turned onto Bricker Street, and soon after onto Stony Road.

David parked his bike in the rack outside Pebble Creek Ice Cream. Matt dumped his bike on the sidewalk, along with his helmet. "What flavour are you going to have?" Both boys were aiming to try every flavour in the store by the end of the summer.

"Mocha Supreme Almond Fudge," said David.

"Hey," Matt objected, "isn't that two flavours?"

"So, is there a rule against two flavours?"

In the corner of the ice cream store, a video game beeped and bonked. Matt and David faced the rows of colourful tubs behind the cold glass wall of the freezer.

"Hey, Martha," Matt said to the teenager

behind the counter. "I didn't know you worked here."

"I just started. The variety store wasn't giving me enough hours. This is a way cooler place to work anyway."

Matt ordered Peanut Butter Ripple on a sugar cone. David went for Strawberry Banana.

"What happened to Mocha Supreme Almond Fudge?" Matt asked.

"Another time," said David.

The boys sat on the bench outside, slurping and munching their ice cream. The striped awning above them gave little relief from the scorching heat, but their ice cream soon cooled them off nicely from the inside.

Across the street, in the window of The Purple Flamingo, two teenagers were getting their hair done. One appeared to be getting the molded purple hairdo that gave the place its name. The head of the other customer was starting to look like lime-green cotton candy.

A tall teenager with pink hair, green lips, and

jagged lines painted around her eyes walked into the funky hair salon. "Hey, isn't that Rapture?" said David.

"Yeah, that's her," Matt answered. "She works there." He licked a creamy drip from the side of his cone. "I still can't believe she's Mr. Grubb's granddaughter, can you?"

"After finding out the creepy old guy set up that treasure hunt," David said, "I'd believe anything."

"What kind of hair style would suit *him*, do you think?" Matt wondered out loud.

"How about a Towering Inferno, to make him even taller?"

Matt laughed. "It would give him a bit of colour, too. Come to think of it, your boring black hair could do with a bit of jazzing up too."

"Mr. Grubb with orange hair," imagined David. "What a concept."

With his tongue Matt stopped another blob of ice cream from dripping down his cone. "So, David," he said, "you're a brainer. How can I come up with big whack of dough in a hurry?"

"You could rob a bank," David suggested. "What do you want? A year's supply of Purple Flamingo hairdos?"

"Very funny. Seriously though, there's this awesome Supercycle Impulse in the window of Silver Streak. It's a perfect bike, but it costs a mint."

"Can't you talk to your parents?"

"No. We're kind of broke right now."

"What about saving up? How much do you make on your paper route?"

"About twenty dollars a week."

"So, at twenty dollars a week, it would take you —" David frowned as he tried to figure out the answer.

"— forever," Matt said. "You don't have to be great at math to work that out. Besides, the paper is switching to all adult carriers at the end of the month, and I'll be out of a job then."

Finishing their ice cream, the boys pondered Matt's problem.

"Hey, I know." David popped the tip of his cone into his mouth, went inside, and came out with a copy of the *Pebble Creek Post*. "I saw this yesterday. Listen." He read from the newspaper:

This year is Pebble Creek's centennial year. On August 2nd Stony Road will be closed to traffic so that residents may celebrate the town's 100th birthday.

"So? It'll probably just be a bunch of boring speeches and old pictures."

David folded the paper. "Okay. If you don't care about the bike prizes being offered, I won't read any more."

"What?" Matt grabbed the newspaper. "Where'd you see that?"

David pointed to the box at the bottom of the page.

2

"BIKE PRIZES," DAVID said. "Right here."

"Read it."

"Why don't you?"

"Don't bug me," said Matt.

David read the last part of the announcement in the *Pebble Creek Post*:

> *As well as displays and demonstrations regarding different aspects of life in the community over the years, a Grand Parade of Bikes will be open to residents of all ages. There will be games for kids aged four to seven. Eight- to ten-year-olds are eligible to enter the Great Bike Race.*

Grand prizes — a Supercycle Impulse FS-MTB and a Night-Rider bicycle — will be donated by Silver Streak Cycle & Sports, in addition to some smaller prizes.

"Well, good-bye, beat-up old bike!"

David laughed. "You think you're going to win a race with that old wreck?"

"You haven't seen what this baby can do." In a smooth set of moves that he had down pat, Matt threw on his helmet, straightened his crooked seat, hopped on his bike before the seat could slip out of place again, and took off.

"Wait up!" hollered David.

At the corner of Stony Road and Sandhurst, Matt slammed on his brakes, shooting up a spray of coarse gravel. David skidded to a halt behind him.

Matt beamed. "Not bad for an old clunker, eh!"

"Not bad," David admitted. "But watch this." He hurtled along Sandhurst with Matt hot on his tail. At almost the same instant, the battered blue bike and the almost-new red one spun around the corner onto Booth Street.

On David's front lawn, both boys collapsed, laughing.

At the house next to David's, the screen door squeaked open slowly, and onto the rickety porch stepped Mr. Grubb. The old man dropped his large frame into a weather-worn wicker chair.

"Is he mad 'cause we were laughing?" David whispered.

"He always looks mad, remember," Matt said. "It's because of how his face pulls down at the sides." Matt tugged on his own cheeks to demonstrate. "And the way his big bushy eyebrows poke out." He twisted his own brows and tried to look mean.

David rolled over in the grass to stifle another laugh.

Seeing Mr. Grubb reminded Matt that he hadn't yet taken David to his secret place, as he'd planned to the day he found out it had been Mr. Grubb's secret place, too, when he was a boy.

"Hey, come with me," he said. "I want to show

you that place by the river."

David said. "I thought maybe you'd changed your mind about that."

"No. After my mom called me home that day when I first said I was going to take you, I kind of forgot about it, that's all."

As they pedalled into the ravine, Matt hoped it wasn't stupid, taking David to this place that none of the other kids knew about. He'd never taken anyone else there, not even his best friend, Mike Lennox. And he'd only just started being friends with David this summer, when everyone else was on holidays.

Matt led David into the shadiest part of the ravine, then off the main path onto a dirt one. Over a bumpy section of ground his bike rattled. David's bike took the bumps more easily. The path dipped down suddenly, then back up. At the top Matt turned sharply to the right. The path was so narrow that it almost disappeared.

"Yikes," David complained, "the weeds keep grabbing at my pedals."

"Don't come in if you don't want to."

"Are you kidding? Secrets are awesome."

Near a big boulder, Matt dropped his bike into the bushes. "Leave your bike here."

David leaned his bike beside Matt's. Matt shoved aside some ferns and slid down the sandy bank. David followed. And there they were — where Matt always went when he had some thinking to do, or when he wanted to be alone.

Around the pebbly little beach at the base of the curved bank, trees leaned out over the river. Cool water gurgled over the stones. Splashes of sunlight danced through the leaves and sparkled on the river's surface. Being here was like being in a different world from the hot dusty streets of town.

"Wow," said David.

In the cool sand of the bank, Matt wriggled his body until it formed a comfortable hollow. He was glad being here was as big a deal for David as it was for him.

David stood at the edge of the quiet river, the water sliding by the toes of his runners.

"I like the part of the river by the wooden bridge," he said, "but this sheltered spot is even better. Thanks for bringing me here."

Matt stood up and skipped a stone across the water. Ripples wavered out from each spot where the stone touched. "Do you know how to skip stones, David?"

"You really still think I only know how to read and do math, don't you?" David picked up a flat piece of shale and hurled it. It bounced several times across the water before it sank.

"Not bad," Matt commented, "but you'll never beat my record."

"How many skips have you done?"

"Fourteen."

David threw another stone. It skipped nine times.

Matt heaved a larger stone into the river. Large enough that its splash erased all sign of David's nine-skipper.

"I should be getting home for supper," Matt said.

The boys clambered up the bank.

"Does this place have a name?" David asked.

"What? Here? No."

"What do you think of … Secret Sands?"

Matt grimaced. "You really want to know?"

David stopped near the top of the cliff. "Then how about… The Place?"

"Why does it need a name?" objected Matt. "It never needed one before."

"I was just thinking, now that two of us know about it — three counting Mr. Grubb — maybe there should be a code word for it."

"Yeah. Maybe."

"How about *Mistikos Topos*?"

"What's that?"

"It's Greek for 'secret place'."

Yanking his bike out of the bushes, Matt paused. "Okay, David. If you really think we need a name, that thing you said doesn't sound too lame."

When Matt and David got back to Booth Street, the moving van was still parked outside Sam's old house. A girl in red shorts and a T-shirt was shifting a large box out of the back of the truck.

"I wonder if she'll be in our class in September," said David.

"Who cares?" Matt said. "Girls always act like they know everything, and they're good at all the wrong things. Worse than you, even."

The girl in red shorts got a grip on the large box and started toward the house.

David called out to her, "Hey! What grade are you in?"

Without even glancing in the boys' direction, the girl carried her box into the house, her blond ponytail bouncing perkily back and forth behind her.

"Great," declared Matt. "Not just a girl in Sam's house, but a snob, too."

3

THE NEXT MORNING, as Matt polished off his third bowl of cornflakes, there was a knock at the door.

"That'll be David," he said.

Buttering a piece of toast, Matt's mom asked, "What do you boys have planned this morning?"

"Thought we'd go play on Mr. Grubb's computer for a while."

"Oh, good. That poor man doesn't get enough company. He'll be happy to see you, I'm sure."

But it wasn't David at the door.

"Lennox! What are you doing here? I thought you were at your cousin's till next week!"

Lennox was Matt's best friend. He always

reminded Matt of the kid with the cloud of dust around him in the comics, only Lennox was darker-skinned and bulkier.

"My cousin got sick, so I had to come home early," Lennox said.

"That's too bad."

"He was a bore anyway." Lennox drifted into the kitchen. "Kind of like that nerdy guy at school — you know, David Varvarikos?" Lennox pretended he was reading a book and picking his nose at the same time. Finished his imitation, he grabbed an orange from the bowl on the table and started peeling it. "So, what's been doing around here?"

Matt couldn't think of a single answer that wouldn't mean admitting he had been playing with "that nerdy guy at school." "Nothing much."

"Wanna go throw some balls around at the schoolyard?"

"Sure." Matt wolfed down the last of his corn-flakes and headed outside. He brushed the cobwebs from his baseball mitt.

His mom said, "Change of plans, Matt?"

"Yeah, we're going to the schoolyard." Inside his head Matt pleaded with his mother not to make a big deal of it.

"What else was up this morning?" Lennox asked.

"Nothing important. Let's go."

Whap! Fling! Whap! It felt good being back on the baseball field. Feeling the ball smack into his mitt. Putting all his strength behind the ball to send it soaring through the air. Through the years Matt and Lennox had been friends, they'd spent a lot of hours playing ball in this field — from when the spring mud dried until the snow fell again, and as late into summer evenings as the sun would allow. Matt wiggled his hand inside the warm leather glove, ready to make a catch. *Whap!*

Matt was throwing the ball to Lennox when he noticed David. He was outside in his yard, just beyond the fence at the edge of the baseball field. David waved. Matt looked quickly at Lennox to see if he'd noticed.

Good. Lennox had his eye on the ball. But Matt couldn't wave back to David without Lennox seeing.

Turning his back on Matt, David began pulling pegs and poles from a tent — the tent where the two boys had spent several nights together in the past warm week or so. Beside Matt, the ball thunked to the ground.

"Hey, what gives?" Lennox called across the field. "That should have been easy."

"Nothing." Matt picked up the ball and lobbed it back to Lennox.

Maybe he should just tell Lennox about him and David, how they'd kind of become friends. After all, if David were here now, the three boys could have some batting practice.

Except David wasn't much use at batting. He wasn't much good at catching or pitching either. Besides, Matt knew what Lennox would say if he were to suggest having David join them — *What! Play ball with that loser?*

When Matt again let the ball sail past, he

shuffled across the dusty field to fetch it. He was glad Lennox was back. He had missed playing ball. But he liked David now, too. It felt bad ignoring him.

"Are you going to throw that thing?" hollered Lennox. "Or are you trying to hatch it?"

Matt threw the ball. It spun high over Lennox's head. Impossibly high. "Sorry," he called. "Guess I'm kind of out of practice."

Lennox scuffed his sneaker in a patch of hard dirt. "Wanna go have an ice cream instead, then?"

"I just remembered, there's something I've got to do."

"No problem," Lennox said sarcastically. "I'm your best friend, and I've been gone for almost two weeks, but you just go ahead and do whatever it is you've got to do." Lennox scooped up his ball and took off across the field.

Matt thought about following him. But Lennox was moving fast and soon Matt was standing alone in the empty field.

When he got to David's house, David was

rolling up the tent. Matt bent down to help. "Never mind that," David said. "I can do this myself."

Matt plunked himself in the hammock. He tossed aside a book David had left there. "Do you want to go to Mr. Grubb's?"

"Not right now."

"Why not?"

David shrugged.

"Come on," Matt argued. "I gave up a ball game with Lennox so we could go."

"You don't have to hang around with me now," David said. "I knew things would go back to how they were before, once your real friends came back."

"Just because Lennox is back doesn't mean we can't still be friends, too," Matt said. But was that true? When he thought about what Lennox would say about it, he got a horrible, sinking feeling in the pit of his stomach.

David said, "You don't really believe that, do you?" He shoved the last of the tent poles into their nylon bag.

"I don't honestly know," Matt answered. "But I do know that I want to go over to Mr. Grubb's place. With you. We can tell him about — what is it? — *Mistiko*?"

David smiled. "*Mistikos Topos*." He lugged the tent to the storage shed.

Fortunately, Lennox was nowhere in sight when Matt and David emerged from David's yard.

Their steps slowed as they approached Mr. Grubb's rickety porch. The sudden rustle of ivy on the side of the house made Matt's heart thump beneath his T-shirt. The bottom step creaked, and he stifled a nervous giggle. There were always rumours that Mr. Grubb had bodies buried in his garden. Sometimes there were strange sights and smells around his house that suggested they might be true. But Mr. Grubb was harmless, really, Matt reminded himself. And a chance to play the cool games that the old man had on his top-of-the-line computer was more than worth having to put up with a few butterflies flitting around in his stomach.

David tapped at the door.

No answer.

He tried the handle. It wasn't locked. "Should we go ahead in?"

Matt shrugged. "He did say to come back anytime."

Then, behind the screen door, Matt saw a note.

NO COMPUTER CLUB TODAY.
HARD DRIVE CRASHED.
— MR. ARCHIBALD GRUBB

David said, "Guess there's no reason to stay, then. Right?" As he turned to go, Matt grabbed him by the sleeve.

"Yes, there is."

"Are you crazy? With no computer, what's the point?"

"I can't explain it," Matt said, "but something tells me I should go in. And you, too."

David sighed. "I sure hope you know what you're doing."

4

MATT AND DAVID stepped inside. The screen door sprang shut behind them.

After being in the bright sunshine outside, it seemed very dark in the musty-smelling hallway. As Matt's eyes adjusted, the ancient photos of stern-looking people on the wall soon came into focus.

From a room just off the hall, the old man grumbled, "What are you doing here? Didn't you read my note?"

Matt pulled David with him into the doorway.

Mr. Grubb was rocking gently in a high-backed wooden rocker. His cane was hooked over its arm. Mr. Grubb's bony hands rested on a faded red and yellow afghan that he had spread over his knees. His hair was uncombed and lay in tangled clumps around his unshaven face. His jowly cheeks sagged at the corners of his mouth.

Matt's voice shook a little as he asked, "Is it okay if we visit anyway?"

Mr. Grubb stared at him with glazed eyes. A muscle in his cheek twitched. "Why?"

Matt thought the old man had never looked meaner — not in all the years he and other kids on the street had run away from his waving cane. Stammering an apology, Matt started to back out of the room.

"If you came to visit," Mr. Grubb snarled, "why don't you sit down?"

Matt and David looked at each other. Together they perched on the edge of the hard sofa. Mr. Grubb closed his eyes. The creak of rockers against the hardwood floor was the only sound. That, and the *tick, tick, tick* of a grandfather clock in the corner of the room. When it chimed, Matt jumped. Ten o'clock.

David signalled with his head that they should go. But just then the old man opened his eyes and muttered, "There's nothing wrong with the computer."

"Your note ..."

"Fiddle faddle,"Mr. Grubb snapped. "Forget my note." His shaggy eyebrows twitched.

"We'll go now if you want," David offered bravely. He and Matt stood to leave.

"Just sit."

Matt and David sat.

Again Mr. Grubb rocked. His fingers picked at the wool in the afghan across his lap. A thick photo album lay open on the coffee table in front of him. Matt could see that the page it was opened to contained several pictures of a woman in the wicker chair that sat on Mr. Grubb's front porch. Judging by the wrinkles in her face, she was not much younger than Mr. Grubb was.

Matt suddenly became aware, as he stared at the pictures, that Mr. Grubb was watching him. And he was scowling. Matt felt colour rising in his cheeks. "Who ...?"

In a raspy whisper, Mr. Grubb answered. "My wife."

David blurted out, "There's a Mrs. Grubb?"

Mr. Grubb swallowed and closed his eyes again. "Was."

Again Matt and David looked at each other. Mr. Grubb's bony hands clutched the blanket on his lap. He sat like that for so long that Matt thought perhaps he had fallen asleep. When finally he spoke, it was in a voice so low the boys had to strain to hear.

"Ten years. Too long. Too long, I know. But I can't ... Not today. It was ... ten years ago today. Yes. Gone." Mr. Grubb rubbed his big hands over his face and opened his eyes. He looked startled to see Matt and David sitting there.

"I'm sorry we bothered you today," Matt said.

Mr. Grubb nodded. His face looked hard and fierce. "I put that note on the door because I wanted to be alone."

"I thought we should go away," David said,

"but Matt said we should come and see you."

Matt shot David a withering look.

"Two young boys," Mr. Grubb said, "should not be spending a precious summer day keeping an old geezer company while he feels sorry for himself."

"We don't mind," said Matt.

"Well, I mind." Mr. Grubb's cane clattered to the floor. "I have not imposed on my friends that way in eighty-some years, and I have no intention of starting now."

Matt jumped up and crossed the room to pick up the cane. The first time Mr. Grubb had called him a friend, Matt had found it shocking. A week later, it was still startling.

Matt ran his hand over the glossy bumps and dips in the polished wood of the cane. He looked at the old man with his jowly frown, his spiky eyebrows, and his piercing grey eyes. Somehow — now — he didn't look at all scary.

"Margaret bought me that walking stick on my seventieth birthday."

Matt handed it back to him.

Mr. Grubb smiled. "Thank you, my friend."

There was that word again. *Friend.* Matt shook his head. Was he actually starting to *like* the idea of being this old man's friend?

Too weird!

5

MATT AND DAVID cruised slowly up Booth Street on their bikes. Heat rose off the pavement in shimmering waves.

Lennox called from his front step. "Hey, Matt! What are you doing?"

It was too late to pretend he and David weren't together. Matt took a deep breath. "Just riding. Wanna come?"

Lennox dropped the string he was dangling for his cat. "With *Day-vid*?"

The way Lennox sneered summed up everything he and Matt had ever thought of the quiet boy who only seemed to be interested in school. "Day-vid" was a wimp. A bore. A sissy. And

Lennox was having nothing to do with him.

"Come on, Lennox. Get your bike. We can all go riding." Matt tried hard to make it not sound like the dumbest idea he'd ever come up with.

"Yeah, right," Lennox scoffed. "Ask me again when Mumbles has puppies."

Mumbles rolled over and let out a loud meow.

David muttered, "You don't have to do this, Matt."

"Don't worry about it."

Matt stopped to reconnect his chain, then sped along Sandhurst to the high school. He peeled around the corner into the empty parking lot and began doing a series of jumps over the curbstones.

When David caught up, he said, "No wonder your bike is so wrecked." He zigzagged back and forth between the curbstones.

"Never mind," said Matt. "It's a good bike. And on August second, we'll do just fine."

"Once I've trained to get my speed up," David boasted, "you won't have a chance."

At the edge of the lot Matt halted. "You're entering the race, too?"

"Don't look so shocked. There's plenty of athletic stuff I'm no good at, but bike-riding is my forte."

Just then Lennox whizzed along Sandhurst on his bike. "Hey, David!" he called. "Is that *Greek* school you go to every Saturday? Or *Geek* school?" It was an old joke. Over his shoulder he added, "Guess you'll be going there, too, eh, Matt?"

Matt's stomach churned. He wanted to shout back something clever, but instead he snarled at David. "What are you talking about — *forte?*"

David steered along the white line that separated the parking areas for students and for teachers. "It means I'm good at it."

"So, why don't you just say so, then?"

"I don't need to say anything actually. Soon you'll see for yourself." David's wheels did not waver one bit off the line.

Matt sped up and aimed his bike straight

toward the perfect BMX and its perfect rider, as if he was going to crash right into them. David wobbled off the line and almost fell. At the last possible moment, Matt veered away, laughing. "You didn't really think I'd hit you, did you?"

"Of course not." David's face turned bright red. "It was reflex, that's all."

"Right."

Matt planted his feet on the ground. He picked at the peeling blue paint on the crossbar of his bike. "Look," he said, "I don't know why I did that. Sorry."

"No big deal." David tucked his shirt back into his shorts. "And, you know, if you want to go catch up with Lennox, it's okay," he said. "I'd understand."

"Don't be such a wimp," Matt said. "You should be yelling at me. I was a jerk."

David just shrugged.

Matt shook his head. Exasperated with how easy-going David could be sometimes, he said, "I need an ice cream. Come on. Let's go."

At Pebble Creek Ice Cream, Matt exclaimed, "Martha!" Her plain brown hair had been cut short — shorter than his. What was left of it was pinched into tiny pyramid-shaped tufts all over her head.

"I just needed a change," Martha said. "Do you like it?"

Matt nodded politely, but he was thinking he would never in his whole life figure out girls. Not even if he lived as long as Mr. Grubb.

David read out the list of flavours on the board. "Very Vanilla. Baseball Nut. Pebble Creek Krickle. Cookie Crumble Jumble …" Matt ordered a double scoop of Baseball Nut and Rum 'n' Raisin. David ordered Orange Pineapple and Licorice Spice.

Outside, Matt licked the dent where his two flavours of ice cream met. David nibbled orange ice cream from the top, saving the grey scoop to eat last. Matt made gagging noises and said, "How can you eat grey ice cream?"

David just ignored him.

"It looks like — " Matt made sounds so gross he could hardly stand it himself.

David pulled a book from the deep pocket of his shorts and began to read.

"David," objected Matt, "do you have to do that now?"

"Is there something else I should be doing?"

"Just eating. Ice cream can't taste right if you're reading, too. When you're eating ice cream," Matt explained, "you're supposed to be just goofing off."

"Reading *is* goofing off," David argued.

"Not for me," said Matt. "Listen. Can't you put that book away? It's spoiling the taste of my ice cream."

David shoved his book back into his pocket. "You just don't like books because you're not much good at reading."

"Oh, wow," Matt said. "Can you tell me something else I don't know?"

"Before I knew you, I thought that meant you were stupid," David said. "So all that time before

— when you didn't want to play with me? I didn't want to play with you either."

"Because I'm stupid?"

"I used to think so. But you aren't stupid about important things."

"Gee, thanks." Matt bit the bottom out of his cone, then had to ask, "Important things like what?"

David bit the bottom out of his cone, too. "Like this morning. You knew we should ignore the note and go in to see Mr. Grubb. I didn't know that." He sucked a creamy grey blob through the hole in the tip of his cone.

"Hey, Matt!" Lennox laid some rubber in front of the ice cream store. "Look at this new baseball I just got." He thrust it into Matt's hand. "Wanna go try it out?"

Matt crammed the last of his cone into his mouth. He fingered the ball's red stitching and sniffed its smooth, white leather. "That's a beaut, Lennox." He handed the ball to David to admire.

Lennox snatched it back. To Matt he said,

"Are you planning to hang around with this geek all summer?"

"He's not that bad, Lennox. Can't you just give him a chance?"

"Are you kidding? I've seen this guy throw a ball," Lennox sneered. "Never seen him catch one, though."

"But you should see him — "

David interrupted. "Forget it, Matt." He flipped the empty end of his cone into the garbage basket. "What makes you think I want to hang around with this goof anyway?"

Matt felt the sweet ice cream he had just eaten turning sour in his stomach.

"You going to let that stupid brainer call me names?" Lennox waved his baseball in Matt's face. "I thought we were supposed to be friends."

"We are. Of course we are. But like it or lump it — " Matt shoved aside the ball and stared straight into Lennox's eyes. "David is my friend now, too."

Lennox kicked his bike pedal into place. "Well,

I don't hang around with geeks!" He shoved off down Stony Road. "So, you'd better decide," he hollered, "are you going to be friends with David, or are you going to be friends with me?!"

"Cripes," Matt grumbled. "He's impossible!"

Curled up on the bench, David's nose was buried in his book.

"Ah, cripes!" Matt repeated. "So are you!"

He grabbed his bike from the pavement and tore up Stony Road at top speed. He barrelled across the top of the quarry. Was he shaking because of the rough path, or was it his insides? He couldn't tell.

Who needs either one of them? Matt thought. *Not me!* He bumped across the wooden bridge and headed into the ravine. On the path to *Mistikos Topos,* he heard the familiar grinding sound underneath him.

"Stupid bike!" he yelled. "Stupid friends!" He stopped, and for the millionth time, reattached the nuisance chain and straightened the crooked seat. The seat came off in his hands. Cursing a blue streak, Matt pitched it — hard — into the bushes.

By the side of the river, tears stung Matt's eyes. What good was having two friends he liked if they couldn't stand each other? And what was wrong with him, anyway? Nobody else had any trouble being friends with lots of different people. But it seemed he would have to spend the rest of his stupid life trying to juggle his time between David and Lennox. *If* he could be bothered with either one of them.

In the meantime, he had to win that race and the Supercycle Impulse first prize. His old bike wasn't going to last much longer.

6

MATT TOOK A screw from one of the bins in Harry's Hardware and checked it against the holes in his bike seat. Too fat. He chucked it back into the bin. Out the corner of his eye he caught sight of two people energetically gesturing to each other at the end of the aisle. He looked up from the screws.

It was the new girl and a woman he thought was likely her mother. The girl's mother was moving her hands in the language Matt had once seen someone teaching on TV when he was flipping channels. The girl shook her head no, and signed something back.

So she wasn't a snob, as Matt had thought

when she didn't answer David. She was deaf.

The girl's face and even her body said there was something she wanted — badly. Even though Matt didn't understand the language she and her mother were using, he could tell they were arguing.

When the girl's mother started walking away, her face stiff, the girl tapped her shoulder hard. Her mother turned. The girl repeated her sharp hand movements, but this time it seemed she was almost crying. The girl's mother glanced in Matt's direction.

Embarrassed to be caught staring, Matt looked away.

As Matt chose a screw from a bin, the girl's mother came over to Matt and said, "Hello. Aren't you the boy who lives next door to us?"

Surprised that she could speak, Matt answered, "Yeah, I'm Matt Randall."

The girl's mother signed to her daughter, then said to Matt, "This is Amanda. I'm Sandra Pirie."

Amanda held her hand up in a weak greeting.

Matt didn't need to know sign language to understand she was not very excited about meeting him.

Matt asked the girl's mother, "Don't most deaf people just read lips?"

"Some do, including Amanda to some extent, but it's pretty limited," Mrs. Pirie explained. "ASL — American Sign Language — is more precise. My husband and I decided to learn it so that Amanda has someone she can talk to at home as well as at school."

Matt said, "I don't think anyone at my school knows sign language."

"Amanda will be going to the school for the deaf on the other side of town."

"Oh, yeah."

Amanda tugged her mother's arm, forcing her to look at her angry face. Matt stood by, mystified, as his new neighbours signed to each other. Although they weren't talking in the way Matt thought of as talking, it was obvious that Amanda and her mom were having a real conversation.

Amanda's mom explained to Matt, "Amanda

feels left out if I forget to tell her what I'm saying when I'm talking to a hearing person. She was just reminding me."

As her mother spoke, Amanda pulled a registration form for the bike race off the notice board beside the helmets.

"Is Amanda going to enter the bike race?" Matt asked.

"I'm afraid that's what we've been arguing about. I wish she wouldn't. But why don't you ask her yourself?"

"I don't know how."

"You can probably say more than you think, even without ASL. It would mean a lot to Amanda if you'd try."

Matt glanced around to be sure no one was watching, and stepped a little closer to the deaf girl. When she looked up at him, he pointed to the poster about the race, to her, then back to the poster. Without thinking about it, he raised his eyebrows as if he were asking a question.

Amanda's eyes lit up. She nodded her head.

She signed to her mom, who then said to Matt, "Amanda says I worry too much that everything fun is dangerous. She loves to ride her bike fast, feel the wind in her face. She'll enter the race, she says, no matter what I say."

Boy, Matt thought, Amanda sure was no wimpy girl who let her parents run her life. He smiled in a way he hoped showed that he agreed with her about bike-riding. "Is there a sign for Amanda?" he asked her mother.

Mrs. Pirie signed to her daughter briefly.

Amanda looked at Matt, closed four fingers against her palm, and waggled her hand back and forth. Matt tried to imitate her. Amanda showed him to straighten his thumb more beside his closed fingers.

When Matt got it right, Amanda smiled, and her mom gathered up her curtain rods.

"Bye, Amanda," Matt said, awkwardly making the sign for her name.

Amanda folded the registration form for the race into her pocket and fished out a card. She handed it to Matt. It had her e-mail address printed on it.

Only after Amanda and her mom left the store did it occur to Matt that he had actually been talking to a deaf girl. He couldn't imagine why he'd ever want to e-mail her, but tucked her card in his pocket anyway.

Matt borrowed a screwdriver from the owner of the hardware store, reattached the seat of his bike, then pedalled back toward Booth Street.

Coming up behind Amanda on the ravine path, Matt rang his bell. But of course, she didn't hear it, just like she hadn't heard David call to her when she was unpacking the truck. Pulling up alongside Amanda, Matt said to her mother, "Couldn't it be dangerous for Amanda to go in a race if she can't hear?"

"It could be," Mrs. Pirie answered. "But Amanda has proven to be quite the little hotshot rider, and she really wants to do it." Mrs. Pirie shrugged. "But I insist she wears her helmet."

"Yeah, my mom makes me wear one, too."

Again, Matt had to admire Amanda's guts, standing up for what she wanted. And it was easy to be pleased for her that she was entering the race. It was a cinch she didn't have a chance of winning.

Amanda waved and Matt pedalled on. He slowed down near the white frame house where Lennox lived.

"Hey, Matt," Lennox called from under a blanket hung like a tent over the porch railings. "Have you seen this?"

Matt partly wanted to stay mad at Lennox for how he had treated David earlier. But it was hard to stay mad at your oldest friend. He had known Lennox since they'd both got in trouble in Kindergym for not taking turns with other kids on the mats. Every year at school they'd kept each other company in the slowest reading groups, too. And when Matt was stuck at home last year with chicken pox, Lennox was the one friend who always came by with gummi eyeballs or Wurmz N Dirt candy, or with comics and a new joke.

Matt dropped his bike on the lawn. "Come see what?" He crawled into Lennox's tent. It was kind of babyish, and the blanket wasn't big enough to hang all the way down the sides, but it made good shade on a sweltering day.

Lennox pointed to a page in his comic book. "If you send away popsicle wrappers, you can get all these neat prizes — baseball caps, bats, a telescope. And look, even a bike."

"Yeah, right. If you eat six popsicles every day from now till you get to high school, you might have enough for a bike."

"So?" Lennox argued. "You don't need as many for the telescope, and you can go around collecting them from other people, and ..."

"You collect popsicle wrappers to get what *you* want, Lennox. *I'm* planning to win the Supercycle Impulse in the bike race."

"What bike race?"

Oops. "Nothing," Matt said quickly.

"Forget 'nothing'," pressed Lennox. "What bike race?"

In a last-ditch attempt to get Lennox to forget about it, Matt said, "Just some dumb thing David saw in the paper."

Lennox started rifling through the recycling box full of newspapers and then flipping through pages until he came to an announcement of Pebble Creek's anniversary celebrations.

"Qualifying heats are tomorrow," he said. "They're going to narrow all the entrants so only five kids each age go in the final race."

"You're not going to enter, are you?"

"Sure," Lennox said. "It beats trying to come up with twenty-five hundred popsicle wrappers."

Darn. Thanks to Matt's own big mouth, he would now have one more excellent bike-rider to beat out.

Lennox's babysitter called from the other room, "Speaking of popsicle wrappers, Michael, how about getting that pigpen you call a bedroom cleaned up before your mother gets home from work?"

Lennox groaned. Whether it was because he

hated cleaning his room or being called by his first name, Matt couldn't tell. Probably both.

"Guess I'll see you at the qualifier, *Michael*." Matt teased him. He picked up his bike from the scorched grass.

It was rotten of him to wish Lennox wasn't entering the race. But he needed the Supercycle Impulse way more than Lennox did. And Lennox was probably his toughest competition.

From across the street Mr. Grubb waved his cane. Matt waved back.

"May I ask you to do me a favour, Matt?"

Matt dumped his bike by the front porch and followed Mr. Grubb into the cool house. When the door closed behind him, Matt realized he had never been in Mr. Grubb's house without David before. He felt a shiver tickle up his spine and down again.

7

MATT TOLD HIMSELF not to be silly. Wasn't it just yesterday he was saying to David how different Mr. Grubb was from the mean, old man they thought he was? And saying he'd felt good that Mr. Grubb considered him a friend?

"There is a box of photographs up in my attic," Mr. Grubb said, "that I would like to have down here."

The attic? With its tiny, little window that looked all smeary, as if fingers had scrabbled against it from the inside?

"My granddaughter, Rapture, usually drops by after work," Mr. Grubb continued. "I was going to get her to go up there for me. But I wonder —

would you mind getting them for me now? Our talk this morning has made me quite anxious to retrieve them."

"You want me to go up in your attic?"

"If you wouldn't mind. I'd get the box myself, but I was a bit shaky last year, coming down those steep stairs. It's a red and gold striped box, I think. It's not heavy, it's just …"

"I'll get it," Matt said. He followed the old man up the stairs. Partway up, Mr. Grubb turned.

He seemed even bigger than he usually did, peering down at Matt from the extra height the stairs gave him. His bushy eyebrows cast scary shadows across his face. What if everything people said about the old man and the bodies buried in his yard was true? About bodies buried in his yard? For an instant Matt considered pretending to remember that his mom wanted him at home for something.

But before he could speak, Mr. Grubb said, "I very much appreciate your doing this for me, Matt."

In the middle of a small room on the second floor stood two plastic bodies without heads. Weird paraphernalia — beakers and tubing, coloured bottles, pieces of twisted metal — lined the shelves on one wall and littered the floor. Inside the closet were the stairs to the attic. Matt climbed the stairs and shoved aside the board at the top. He stepped up through the hole into the attic.

The tiny, square attic window looked even grimier than it did from the street. It took a minute for Matt's eyes to grow accustomed to the dim light.

Matt made his way into the room one slow step at a time. It was absolutely crammed with boxes and trunks and shelves. Cobwebs stretched across Matt's face. He brushed them aside. A high shelf jammed with books held no box with gold and red stripes. Matt crept on past. Which way should he go now, through the maze of stuff that had accumulated over the years?

Under a sheet of dusty plastic, a rack of old suits and dresses stood at attention. Matt half expected them to lean forward so they could examine the curious, 21st-century creature in their midst. Below him, Matt heard Mr. Grubb's muffled voice calling as if from a great distance. "Someone is at the door," he was saying, "I'll be back in a minute."

Behind the rack, under the window, Matt came upon another shelf. On top of it sat a gold and red striped box. As he went to get it down, he noticed beside him a dark sheet of plastic thrown over an oddly familiar shape.

Crash! The noise reverberated through the attic. Before he could stop it, a strangled cry escaped Matt's mouth. Before Matt could bring himself to face whatever had made the startling noise, he again heard Mr. Grubb's muffled voice. "Sorry, Matt, I knocked over one of Rapture's mannequins. I didn't mean to scare you."

"It's okay," Matt called down. "You didn't."

He brushed dust from the box he knew Mr. Grubb was waiting for. But he was still curious about the mysterious grey shape huddled between the shelf and the clothes rack.

Walking around it, Matt touched the odd bumps that gave the dustcover shape. He crouched down and slowly lifted the edge of the plastic.

He saw a tire. Spokes. A pedal.

He was right. He pulled the plastic cover right off the bicycle he had discovered. Its steel frame was a flat, dark blue. It had no chrome or decals to jazz it up. There were no gears or handbrakes, either. Matt ran his hands over the dull heavy handlebar and squeezed the leather grips.

Could this have been Mr. Grubb's bike when he was young? He could enter it in the Grand Parade of Bikes at Pebble Creek's centennial.

"Did you find it, Matt?"

The box. Mr. Grubb was waiting for the box of photos.

Matt lifted its lid to be sure it was what Mr. Grubb wanted. He carried it carefully past the old bicycle and other dusty relics. He rested it against each stair in front of him as he backed down out of the attic.

"Shall I take that now?" Mr. Grubb offered.

"I can do it," insisted Matt. He was dying to talk to Mr. Grubb about the bike.

"Just put it in the kitchen, then," Mr. Grubb said. "Thank you."

When Matt saw who was sitting in the kitchen, just as if she belonged there, the old bike and the possibility of entering it in the Grand Parade went right out of his mind.

"Amanda?"

"You two have met?" asked Mr. Grubb.

"Yeah, but..." How had this new girl — who couldn't even hear or speak — made friends with Mr. Grubb already?

Matt couldn't explain why, but he suddenly felt terribly jealous, even possessive of this man who was such a new friend. "How do you two know each other?" he asked.

Mr. Grubb explained. "I spotted Amanda looking at her baseball cards in front of her house. I started to tell her about my collection, but she wouldn't answer. I assumed she was ignoring me because she'd been taught not to speak to strangers."

"Didn't you know she was deaf?"

"How would I know that?"

Matt remembered when David had called to Amanda as she was unloading the truck. Of course, no one would know she was deaf until they tried to talk to her.

"Her mother was nearby," Mr. Grubb continued. "I told her I had a very old baseball card collection that her daughter might be interested in seeing, and that she was welcome to come see it anytime. And here she is."

Matt felt another little pang. Because of how easily the new girl had connected with Mr. Grubb, and because he wouldn't have minded seeing the old baseball card collection himself.

"I think Mrs. Pirie wasn't too keen on Amanda coming to visit when they'd only just met me."

"Amanda is very determined," Matt said.

"Yes. And I understand your mother kindly vouched for my character."

Amanda glanced up from the rows of baseball cards arranged on the table in front of her. She took a few more from the box beside her.

Matt said to Mr. Grubb, "I never knew you collected baseball cards."

"Have a look. I've got cards going back for years."

Amanda was laying out the cards according to which teams the players were on. She seemed also to be arranging them by age. Old cards were at the top of her arrangement, more modern ones toward the bottom. She looked up at Matt, and pointed, first to him and then at the cards.

What did she mean? She couldn't be asking if the cards were his. She knew they belonged to Mr. Grubb. So she wasn't offering them to Matt either.

Matt shrugged and shook his head to say he didn't understand.

Amanda reached into her pocket and pulled out a small pad of paper and a pencil. She wrote a note and showed it to Matt. It said, *Do you have a baseball card collection too?*

Matt shook his head.

Mr. Grubb pawed through a small stack of cards. He took Amanda's pad and wrote, *My oldest card.* He handed it back to her, along with his 1927 card of New York Yankees first baseman Lou Gehrig.

Amanda's eyes and mouth opened wide. Smiling, she gave him a thumbs-up.

For a few more minutes, Amanda and Mr. Grubb looked at baseball cards, using gestures and facial expressions to indicate favourite players and favourite baseball moments. Matt wondered how Amanda got to be such an expert on baseball? She was turning out to be kind of okay, for a girl. Still, he couldn't help being a bit miffed that the box he'd gone to such trouble to bring down from the attic didn't seem to matter any more.

As if she'd just thought of a brilliant idea, Amanda suddenly started to act out opening up a newspaper and reading it. She made a little hook with her finger.

"I have one here somewhere," Mr. Grubb said.

He nodded to Amanda before going off to get it.

Matt pointed to Amanda's pad and pencil, and she handed them to him. Unsure of his spelling, Matt was much slower than Amanda at writing his message. Finally he handed her his question: *What do you want the paper for?*

You'll see.

When Mr. Grubb returned with the *Pebble Creek Post*, Amanda spread it out over the baseball cards. She turned to a page about the upcoming anniversary celebration and pointed to a notice that read:

> *The residents of Pebble Creek are invited to*
> *submit their collections — stamps, coins,*
> *rocks, butterflies, whatever — to the library.*
> *The most interesting collections will be dis-*
> *played there, inside glass cases, for one week.*

"Not many people would be interested in these old cards," said Mr. Grubb, and wrote the words on Amanda's pad, too.

"We were," Matt said.

Amanda took her pad back from Mr. Grubb and wrote, *I can set up your cards to look so beautiful that everyone will want to see them.*

Mr. Grubb laughed and gave Amanda's pony-tail a gentle tug.

The open newspaper reminded Matt of what he'd been so keen to say when he came down from the attic. "There's something else," he said, "upstairs in the attic."

With his puzzled expression, Mr. Grubb's eyebrows spiked out at odd angles.

"David read about it," Matt sputtered on, searching the paper for some mention of the parade. "For the anniversary. It's got to be here somewhere."

Mr. Grubb chuckled. "Slow down, old boy. What on Earth are you talking about?"

Matt heaved a sigh and started again. When he had told Mr. Grubb about both the Great Bike Race and the Grand Parade of Bikes, the old man asked, "But what does this have to do with me?"

"The bike in your attic has to be the oldest one in Pebble Creek, right? And no one will expect you to still have it. You've got to enter it in the parade, Mr. Grubb."

"Why, I'd forgotten it was up there." The old man laughed a laugh that seemed to start in his belly and explode from his whole face. "My friend," he said, "I do believe you're right!"

8

MATT'S MOM STUFFED a handful of bills behind the canisters on the counter. "Guess you're glad to have Lennox back from his cousin's," she said.

"I guess so. He's being stupid about David though." Flipping through channels with the TV remote, Matt poked at his cornflakes. He stopped flipping when he chanced on the station where ASL was being taught.

"If you don't mind my saying so, you were pretty stupid about David yourself for quite a while," Matt's mom said. "Give Lennox a chance. He'll come around."

Matt shoved aside his bowl. "Hope so. I gotta go now. Tryouts for the race are this morning."

Police were redirecting traffic along the streets where the tryouts would take place. Crowds of hopeful racers were gathering in the field alongside the high-school parking lot.

What a lot of kids, Matt thought. Beating Lennox would be only part of his problem. Why, it was possible that he might not even make it past the qualifier. Waiting for his age group to be called, Matt plunked himself down on the stubbly grass beside his tired, old bike.

Soon David showed up and leaned his bike against the wall of the school. With his shirt neatly tucked into his tidy shorts, he sure did look like a geek. No one but David would be caught dead in clothes like his. Matt watched David standing there and half expected to see him pull a book from his pocket. What had ever made him think that they could actually be friends?

When David glanced in his direction, Matt pretended to look for a four-leaf clover in the clump by his foot. He told himself he was too worried about the tryouts to feel like talking to anyone.

There were two parts to the qualifiers. While one bunch of kids did speed tests along Sandhurst, others had to maneuver their bikes around a series of obstacles in the parking lot. They lost points for wavering off a line or hitting a pylon. As each group of sweaty kids cleared out of the competition area, it was obvious which ones had and hadn't qualified for the big race.

Matt watched a kid trudge off the parking lot with his bike, his hopes of entering the race dashed. *Please, please, don't let that be me!* Matt thought. *I need that Supercycle Impulse!*

When the announcement was made for Matt's age group to gather, he wheeled his bike over to the lot. The organizers divided up the kids. He, Lennox, and David were all in the group that would start with the maneuvering test. An official lined everyone up and explained what to do.

David started out first along the white line. Matt followed, and a dozen or so other kids came along behind him. As David steered cleanly along the line, it reminded Matt of their riding together for practice, here and through the ravine. Thinking of the ravine led to thoughts of the place by the river that David had made up that mysterious Greek name for.

He was a bit weird, David was, but he was also a good friend. Lennox would probably never understand that, and yet Lennox was a good friend, too.

Clunk. Oh, no! As Matt was following the twisting path, his back wheel had bumped an orange pylon. Such a stupid mistake! It could cost him his spot in the race. He'd have to make up for it on the speed test.

More than a dozen kids lined up with Matt at the starting line. At the signal, his bike leaped forward like a racehorse at the starting gate. Matt barrelled along Sandhurst at top speed, neck and neck with two other riders. He pedalled harder, and harder still, until he was ahead of everyone, but only by a wheel.

From out of nowhere it seemed, Lennox flew up beside him, and then out ahead. As soon as he had passed Matt, his front wheel turned — right in front of Matt's!

Matt had to swerve to avoid hitting him. It took all his wits to keep from sliding into the gravel at the side of the road. *I thought we were supposed to be friends. Isn't that what you said, Lennox?* Well, what kind of friend — ?

Back on track, Matt poured on everything he had. He didn't come in first, but he finished ahead of Lennox by seconds.

Matt's heart pounded as he waited for the officials to tabulate the results. Sweat poured down his face.

Before the qualifiers' names were even read out, David rode off. Matt figured he must know he hadn't made it, and actually felt sorry for him.

"Entering the race on August second," one of the organizers shouted into a loud speaker, "will be — in alphabetical order — Tanya Di Angelo…"

How come girls always had to act so surprised whenever they did well at something?

"… Mike Lennox …"

Matt knew exactly where in the crowd the creep was, but he refused to look at him.

"… Amanda Pirie …"

No way! Mrs. Pirie signed to Amanda that she'd made it into the race. It was hard to tell if her mother was pleased or not, but Amanda was jumping up and down.

Matt squeezed the worn grips on his handlebar. Only two more names to go.

"…Matt Randall… "

Yes! Lennox was making his way through the crowd toward him.

"… and David Varvarikos."

David! He'd made it and wasn't even around to find out.

"Hey, Matt!" Lennox called.

Matt hopped on his bike and pushed off to find David and tell him the good news. No way was he waiting around to talk to the biggest rat in Pebble Creek.

When Matt reached the quarry path, David was just crossing the wooden bridge.

"David!" Matt called.

David glanced back over his shoulder and started pedalling faster.

"Wait up, Matt!" Lennox called from behind. "It wasn't how it looked!"

Forget it, thought Matt. *I know who my real friends are.* He chased David over the wooden bridge and onto the path into the ravine. "David, wait!"

David sped out of sight, but Matt pumped hard, trying to catch up. With Lennox not far behind, he caught a glimpse of David turning onto the side path.

Near the boulder in the bushes, Matt dumped his bike by David's. He slithered through the dense ferns and down the bank. Seconds later, Lennox's voice called from above, "Matt?"

Matt and David shoved their backs against the sandy bank.

"Sorry," mouthed David. "I didn't know he was following you."

More quietly than a whisper, Matt muttered,

"Go away, go away, go away."

"Wherever you are, Matt," Lennox called, "I didn't mean to cut you off. Honest."

He sounded sorry. Sad, too, almost.

"Can't we be friends still? Come on, Matt. I know you're around here somewhere."

David scuffed his shoe in the sand. "Do what you want," he whispered. "It's your place."

Matt wanted to scream, *I don't know what I want!*

Solving that problem, the bushes above Matt's head rustled, and Lennox came sliding down the bank. He landed squarely between Matt and David.

"Gee," Lennox said, "I never knew this place was here."

"You weren't supposed to." Matt got up to splash cool water on his face, then plunked back down in the sand.

"I always thought this path was a dead end. How come you never showed me it before?"

Matt shrugged. "It was a secret."

"Seems like *he* knew about it."

"Lennox, maybe it's time you started getting used to the fact that things have changed around here since you went away to your cousin's."

"Are you saying David's a better friend than me?"

Matt stared into the river. Sunlight glinted off the water gurgling over the rocks.

"Well, we did some stuff that would surprise you."

"Like what?"

"The thing is — " Matt began.

"What?"

"You're going to have a hard time believing some of it."

"What are you talking about?"

"Me and David did this treasure hunt."

"So?"

"It got kind of scary near the end."

"So what?"

"Some of the places we had to go weren't very nice."

"So, big deal."

"I almost couldn't finish," said Matt. "I almost chickened out."

"So, what's your point?"

"To find the treasure, we had to go into the creepiest place of all. And it was David who convinced me to go there."

"Yeah?"

"Yeah. And," Matt warned Lennox, "whether you have the guts to come there with us or not, me and David are still friends."

Lennox dug the heel of his shoe into the sand. "So, what was the treasure?"

"If you want to know," Matt said, "you'll have to come with us to where we found it."

Lennox looked at Matt, then at David. He huffed a baffled sigh. "Okay, okay."

He followed Matt and David away from the river and out of the ravine.

On the way back to Booth Street, Matt said, "Hey, David, I almost forgot to tell you why I was chasing you. You made it. You're in the race on Saturday."

"I am?"

"You, me, Lennox — plus the new girl, Amanda. And someone else, I forget who. We're all going on to the final."

"All right!"

At Mr. Grubb's house, Matt opened the front gate.

"No way!" Lennox declared. "You make all the weird new friends you want. This …" He jabbed his finger toward the big, dark house. "is where I draw the line."

9

WITH ONLY A few days left before the big race, Matt was practising fast turns off Pebble Creek's main drag into the quarry. Each time he took the curve, he tried to slow down less. His back wheel shot up a satisfying spray of gravel with every turn.

As he pedalled up the hill out of the quarry for the sixth time, he heard a clattering of metal and a whoop behind him.

"Forget it," Lennox hollered. "You haven't got a chance of beating me."

"Don't count on it!" By the time Matt got the words out, Lennox had already hurtled past.

Matt practised making his turn again, but his heart wasn't in it, and this time he cruised on through the quarry. At the wooden bridge he stopped, settled comfortably, and dangled his arms through the rails.

From the direction of Booth Street came the whirring of a speeding bike. How had Lennox got down again so fast? Hadn't he been heading up Stony Road just a few minutes before?

It wasn't Lennox. It was another of Matt's competitors.

Amanda smiled down at him as the flash of green metal clattered over the bridge. Back on the path, she did a circle-wheelie and waved.

Everyone, it seemed, was practising something, determined to make their best showing come Saturday. Well, never mind. Matt's bike might be the oldest, most decrepit one racing, but he was also the fastest rider and could do more stunts than anyone else in Pebble Creek.

A moment later, David rode past. "How come you're not riding, Matt? Don't you want to be in shape for the race?"

"I'm in shape. Readier than you'll ever be."

Matt grabbed his bike and headed in the opposite direction to where everyone else seemed to be going.

He *was* in shape. He *was* ready for the race. There was no point in wearing out his bike even worse than it already was, preparing for something he was sure to win. Besides, someone with an older bike than his probably needed some help getting ready for Saturday.

Mr. Grubb was sitting on his front porch with a glass of lemonade. He said, "There's sure a lot of cycling back and forth going on around here today."

Matt sighed. "Getting ready for the big race."

Mr. Grubb lifted his glass to his lips. "There's more lemonade in the fridge. Why don't you go in and help yourself?"

Squished-up lemon halves lay on the counter in the kitchen. Mr. Grubb made the sweetest, tangiest lemonade Matt had ever tasted. He filled a glass with ice cubes and lemonade from the pitcher and went back outside.

When Matt had plunked himself down on the step, Mr. Grubb said, "You've never told me what David thought of our secret place."

"He liked it." The cold glass felt good in Matt's hot hands. His breath fogged up when he went to take a drink. "Lennox knows about it now, too."

"Not much of a secret any more, eh?"

"Nope." Matt set his glass down in the wet circle it had made on the porch floor. "None of us hardly seem like friends anymore either."

"Because of the place by the river?"

Matt shook his head. "It's hard to explain."

But he tried. He was surprised how good it felt to be just sitting quietly in the hot shade with his cool lemonade and his slow-moving friend, talking about what he liked about Lennox and David, and how each of them drove him a bit crazy. He didn't say anything about his fears for Saturday's race. Somehow, sitting with Mr. Grubb, away from the other kids and their bikes, Matt's worry was melting away, like the ice cubes in his glass of lemonade.

Mr. Grubb just listened. He didn't tell Matt things would work out just fine with Lennox and David the way most grown-ups would.

Finally Matt said, "How's your bike? Is it ready for the parade?"

"Rapture brought her down from the attic. Had a dickens of a time, too." Mr. Grubb drained the last of his lemonade from his glass. "She could do with a bit of polishing up. The bike, that is, not Rapture."

Matt laughed. "Feel like doing it now?"

Mr. Grubb pushed himself up from his chair. He leaned for a moment on his cane.

"You okay, Mr. Grubb?"

"Hm? Yes, fine," the old man mumbled. "Just stood up a little too quickly, that's all."

Matt had trouble swallowing the last of his lemonade. It didn't seem that Mr. Grubb had stood up very quickly at all. He followed Mr. Grubb as he shuffled into the house.

The old bicycle was leaning against a wall in the computer room. Mr. Grubb flopped into a chair. "There are rags and polish under the sink in the kitchen," he said.

In the doorway Matt turned to say something. Mr. Grubb was wiping his forehead on his sleeve. Matt left the room without speaking. Something told him that Mr. Grubb would prefer to think Matt hadn't seen how uncomfortable he was.

While Mr. Grubb pointed out spots on his bike that needed polishing, Matt did most of the actual rubbing. He hoped it was just the heat that was bothering the old man. But what if it was hot on Saturday, too? Would Mr. Grubb be up to taking part in the parade?

As if he'd read Matt's mind, Mr. Grubb said, "I may not be able to parade Valerie myself."

"Valerie?"

Mr. Grubb chuckled. "My bicycle," he explained. "Valerie was also the name of a good friend of mine years ago. Way back when we were teenagers. I can't recall quite how it started, but I named my bike after her, during some argument we were having, and it somehow stuck."

Matt didn't want to say he thought naming a bike was weird, not when Mr. Grubb was feeling under the weather. He said, "If you can't go in the parade on Saturday, you know who'd be good?"

"Who?"

"Rapture."

Mr. Grubb's eyebrows sprang to life. "Rapture? I hardly think my granddaughter is the old-fashioned bicycle type."

"That's the point. You put this duded up, modern-day teenager right beside your old bike, and it looks even more antique than ever. And you could ask her to get her hair done in The Purple Flamingo's wildest style, too."

"But we want people to notice the bicycle," Mr. Grubb pointed out, "not Rapture."

Matt dabbed a glob of polish on the rear fender and rubbed it until it gleamed.

"I know," he said at last. "You could get Rapture to dress up like a pioneer so it looks like she travelled forward in time to bring your bike to the Grand Parade."

Mr. Grubb's rumbling laugh filled the room. "Just how long ago do you think I was a boy?" The old man wiped the corners of his eyes on his sleeve. "Why don't you leave that for now, and let me show you some pictures. You will notice, Matt, that when I was your age, there were no dinosaurs in Pebble Creek, or knights in armour, and, no, not even covered wagons."

In one of the photos Mr. Grubb showed Matt, a teenage girl sat on a bench under a tree.

"Is that Valerie?" Matt asked.

"Yup, that's her."

"Did you just like her? Or like-*like* her?"

Mr. Grubb put the lid back on the striped box. "Sometimes, friend, you ask too many questions."

"For my own good?" Matt said.

"For mine." Mr. Grubb chuckled. "I don't think we need to worry about getting Rapture to do that parade for me on Saturday. I'm going to be just fine."

10

BRIGHT YELLOW BANNERS shouted in blue letters: *Celebrating 100 years of Pebble Creek!*

Up and down the streets, throngs of the town's residents mingled. Seniors gathered around a display of historic photographs outside the library, comparing faces and places in the pictures to those around them. Pre-schoolers dangled their fishing lines into an old washtub, trying to snag a magnetic fish that would win them a toy, a book, or a candy. Other young kids threw Velcro balls at a fuzzy target for other small prizes.

All the streets were closed to traffic for anniversary events. The Pebble Creek Ice Cream was selling 21st-century flavours at early 20th-century prices. On the sidewalk in front of Joe's Deli, hot dogs were selling for a dime.

A stage was set up at the corner of Stony Road and Bricker. All the valuable junk that people had accumulated over the years, and wanted to get rid of, would be auctioned off there at midday. And that was where, later, the prizes for the Great Bike Race and the Grand Parade of Bikes would be presented.

It was a perfect day for a race — cooler than it had been for a week, and not nearly as humid. Staff from Silver Streak Cycle & Sports checked that the eager racers gathered with their bicycles at Stony Road and Sandhurst all had the required helmets properly strapped on.

"The starting line for today's race," announced the Silver Streak owner, "is by the entrance to the school parking lot. The course will run from there along Sandhurst to Booth Street, down Booth, through the ravine, then along Bricker to where the road comes out of the quarry. All of these streets are closed to traffic ..."

We know, we know, thought Matt. *Let's just get on with it.*

"… and there are staff posted at various points along the route, should anyone require assistance. Any questions?"

Someone shouted, "Supercycle FS-MTB, here I come!"

Matt eyed the boy and gripped his handlebar as if to say, *Forget it, turkey. I'm the one who's going to win that bike.* He hoped no one noticed him grab for the seat that decided, just then, to try to come unattached.

"We wish you all the best in your race," the announcer said. "Please move now to your starting positions."

The racers lined up on the road at the end of the school driveway. An air of determined competition surrounded them. Because of the deaf girl in the race, officials had agreed to drop a flag as a starting signal, in addition to firing a gunshot.

Matt leaned over his handlebar, ready for the

Go. Sweat trickled down the side of his face. He reached up to wipe it away.

Bang!

They were off. Lennox, Amanda, and the kid with the big mouth took early leads. Matt thrust forward and pedalled hard along Sandhurst. He gained quickly on the flashing fenders ahead of him. Then all his practice taking corners at high speeds paid off.

He leaned into the turn onto Booth, cutting close to the big-mouth as he passed him. Coming out of the turn, Matt surged past Lennox, too. Amanda was still ahead, but he'd lose her on the straightaway — no sweat.

Matt stood up to gain an added burst of speed. He headed off Amanda just before taking the bump from the street onto the path into the ravine.

Thud. Clank!

Matt turned. On the ground lay his battered bike seat. So much for the new screw!

What seemed an army of bicycles barrelled toward him. And Amanda hurtled past.

A quick decision. Forget the seat. Finish the race without it.

He had to widen the gap between himself and the riders fast approaching from behind. He had to regain his lead.

Past the side path to *Mistikos Topos*, Matt pedalled like fury. It was like his legs were screaming at him, "No more!" If only he could rest his muscles — for even five seconds — then he could pour it on hard enough to overtake Amanda for sure.

But try sitting? For even a second? On the bare, steel post where the bike seat was supposed to be? No thanks!

Matt held his legs rigid, allowing himself a couple of seconds to cruise. He would overtake Amanda at the turn onto Bricker, and put all he had left into the final straightaway. His legs trembled. Buckets of sweat poured off him. But there was still a chance.

Amanda lost a bit of headway on the corner. Yes!

But she was still in the lead, flying faster than Matt believed possible! Again he pedalled madly.

But something wasn't right. He wasn't gaining momentum. In fact, he was cruising more slowly with each passing second. From beneath him came the too-familiar, grinding sound of his lousy, stinking chain.

Ah, man! Why now?!

And then his tire hit the edge of the path.

Ordinarily it would be no big deal, but with no seat, no chain, and knees that were wobbling like rubber ... Matt's bike crashed to the ground.

The clatter of what seemed like a hundred bikes charging past drowned out his curses.

Sprawled on the ground, Matt tested each arm and leg, to see if anything was broken. Carefully he sat up. He wrapped his stinging arms around his knees that wouldn't stop trembling, and buried his spinning head in them.

It was over. He had lost the race. The sparkling, blue Supercycle Impulse with eighteen speeds, aluminum rims, and knobby tires would not be his. It would go home with somebody else. Maybe Lennox — or worse, with that loud-mouth kid at the starting line. And Matt's trusty old bike was now beyond repair. Useless. to win that prize, *he* did. Matt hurt, inside and out.

The last whirring and rattling of bikes disappeared around the corner. The only sounds in the ravine were those of Matt's heavy breathing, the faint rustle of leaves overhead, the sympathetic chirping of a few birds. And a familiar voice asking, "Are you okay?"

Uncovering his face, Matt squinted in the bright sun. "Lennox! What are you doing here?"

"I saw you crash," Lennox said. "Man, I thought you were a goner!"

"Get back in the race," Matt cried. "I'm okay!"

"It's too late."

"Ah, Lennox, you should have finished."

Lennox shrugged. "I probably wouldn't have won anyway."

"You had a pretty good chance without me in

there." Matt tried to unfold his battered legs and groaned. He stood up his crumpled bike. Its seat was gone, one of its pedals was broken, and its frame was bent.

"Doesn't look like you'll be riding that bike again," Lennox said. At the sight of the scrapes up the side of Matt's leg and the gouge in his elbow, he grimaced. "Here comes a first-aid guy to get you fixed up."

"Well, I hope he works fast. The parade starts in less than half an hour."

"So? It's just a bunch of little brats and old fogeys, isn't it?"

Matt just sighed. "Take my bike and dump it at my place, would you, Lennox?" To the first-aid attendant he said, "And could we please move it here? I've got to get to that parade!"

11

ALL OUT OF breath, Matt limped onto the parking lot of the gas station. There were bicycles, little kids, and senior citizens everywhere. Mr. Grubb, with David beside him, towered over everyone else.

"What's this?" Mr. Grubb scowled. "A walking bicycle safety lesson to lead off our Grand Parade?"

"I wiped out," Matt said, cradling a bandaged elbow against his side. "I probably would have missed seeing you in the parade if Lennox hadn't been there. After he took my beat-up bike home, he picked me up on his bike and rode me here."

Mr. Grubb grumbled, "Sounds to me like

another accident waiting to happen."

Lennox opened his mouth to speak, but then just looked at the ground instead.

Matt ran his hand over the crossbar of Mr. Grubb's bike. "Well, she looks all ready ..."

"Watch you don't leave fingerprints there, now."

Why, Matt wondered, was he being so testy? "You feeling better than the other day?" he asked.

"I'm fine."

Over by the air pump, a small boy who looked like one of Santa's elves started wailing.

"Don't worry. We can tape it back on," his father assured him. A strip of white crepe paper was spiralling down from the bars of a red bicycle on training wheels. "Your bike will be the best candy cane in the parade."

"So," said Mr. Grubb, "I gather you didn't win your race today?"

"I didn't even finish." Matt sighed. "And my bike's a write-off. I'm going to have to do a ton of work to earn enough to buy a new one."

Looking like he might run off at any second because of Mr. Grubb, Lennox said, "I could give you the popsicle wrappers I've been saving."

"That'd be great, Lennox. Then I'd only have to eat about three million more popsicles to get a bike."

Pebble Creek's librarian moved through the crowd. "The Grand Parade of Bikes will begin in five minutes. Cyclists, please line up according to the numbers you were given when you registered."

The paraders began wheeling their bikes into position.

"Good luck, Mr. Grubb," said Matt. "We'll meet you here when the parade is over."

"No, I don't think so, Matt." Mr. Grubb wiped his sleeve across his forehead. "I want you to walk with Valerie. Please. I need to find some shade."

"But it's not that hot today. And you just said you were feeling okay."

"Go on, now," growled Mr. Grubb. "There's no time to argue."

"It's okay, Matt," said David. "I can stay with Mr. Grubb. And Lennox can, too, if he wants."

Reluctantly Matt took Mr. Grubb's bike. He watched as David shuffled toward the shade with their old-man friend. Matt noticed Lennox hanging back from them, but not as far back as Matt might have expected, especially given Mr. Grubb's mood.

Matt limped along with the well-polished, midnight-blue bike. He was behind a bike that was painted in swirling stripes of pink, orange, and green. An entry from The Purple Flamingo, Matt figured. The skintight bodysuit and upright spikes of hair on its owner matched the colours of the bike.

Slowly, the parade crept past the spectators who lined the sides of the streets. Matt found it amusing that, even though Lennox seemed not to want to get too close to Mr. Grubb, he was curious enough to stay within earshot. Matt also hoped Mr. Grubb was going to be okay.

At the corner of Stony and Sandhurst, the

high-school band went from playing the hard rock refrain of "I Want to Ride My Bicycle" to a lilting "Bicycle Built for Two." Some of the older folks in the crowd started to sing along as the parade streamed past.

Matt was sure Mr. Grubb was okay. He looked as healthy and un-grey today as Matt had ever seen him. It was weird how he had decided so suddenly not to go in the parade himself.

Matt's legs and his most badly scraped arm still hurt. But he forced himself to smile as the line of bikes wound through the school parking lot and past the judges. He owed it to Mr. Grubb to make the best showing he could. He hoped the judges noticed the bicycle's clean lines and the great condition it was in after so many years.

After circling twice past the judges, the parade retraced its route. As Matt approached the gas station, he craned his neck to find Mr. Grubb. With the old man being so tall, it should have been easy.

Matt found him sitting under a tree with

David. Lennox was watching them from a short distance away. He looked as if he might be trying to figure out how it was that this David geek could have got into the bike race, and was gutsier about Mr. Grubb than Lennox himself could ever be.

Matt leaned Mr. Grubb's bike against the tree.

"Thank you, my friend."

"No problem," Matt said. "Are you okay now?"

"Oh, yes. Just fine."

"Hey, Lennox, come here," Matt called.

Lennox looked around as if Matt could have been speaking to another Lennox. Watching his shoes as if they might misbehave if he didn't, he sauntered over.

"I want you to meet someone." Matt pulled Lennox closer. "Mr. Grubb, this is Lennox."

Mr. Grubb put out his hand. "Hello, Lennox."

Lennox slowly stuck out his hand.

As their hands touched, the microphone on the stage let out a piercing shriek. Someone rushed up to adjust sound levels, but by then

Lennox had jumped about six feet out of his skin.

Mr. Grubb laughed a deep bellowing laugh. David laughed, too.

Lennox's face went about ten shades of red. Matt thought he was probably getting ready to clobber David for laughing. But instead, he just shook his head. And when Lennox finally burst out laughing, Matt did, too.

Then one grown-up after another got up onstage to talk about Pebble Creek, about how its streets and buildings had changed over the decades but the spirit of the community hadn't "as shown by the turnout today," and on and on and on. David seemed to be actually listening to the boring speeches. Matt smiled. In some ways, he really was a bit of a geek.

While the speeches droned on, Matt noticed Lennox stealing glances at David. The expression on his face wasn't exactly friendly, but maybe the bitter-enemies stuff between them was finished. Maybe the good stuff Matt had been telling Lennox about David was finally sinking in.

Still, Matt knew things with Lennox and David weren't ever likely to be easy. And thinking of all the yard work and deliveries he would have to do to replace his broken bike made him feel downright sick. Why was he standing here, anyway, waiting for some other kid to go up and receive the bike that should have been his?

Who had won the race? He didn't even know. Everything had happened so fast after he crashed that he hadn't had time to find out. Behind the boring speakers on stage, the prize bikes gleamed in the afternoon sun.

Matt wished suddenly that he was somewhere else. *Anywhere* else. On his porch reading comics. At Mr. Grubb's playing computer baseball. Most of all, he wished he was in his old secret place by the river.

He shifted his weight from one foot to the other as the librarian thanked Silver Streak Cycle & Sports for donating the prizes. "A lock and reflectors will be awarded to the runners-up in the Grand Parade of Bikes," she said. "The top-of-the line Night-Rider mountain bike will go to the owner of the parade bike most admired by the judges. And, of course, the sparkling Supercycle Impulse FS-MTB will go to the winner of the Great Bike Race."

The librarian smiled broadly at the crowd. "The judges have just presented me with the envelopes bearing the names of today's winners."

When the elf with the candy-cane bike strode onto the stage to receive his reflectors, the crowd roared with laughter. There was a lock and polite applause for a lady whose bike was decorated to represent all the shops on Pebble Creek's main street. Matt thought the huge salami hanging from her handlebar was a bit much.

"We will now present the grand prizes. First, to the winner of the Great Bike Race." The librarian made a big show of opening the envelope. "Would Amanda Pirie please come up to receive her prize?"

12

AMANDA'S MOM GAVE her a little push toward the stage. Amanda beamed. That she couldn't hear what was being said clearly didn't matter. She had won the Supercycle Impulse FS-MTB. And she knew it. As Amanda proudly wheeled the bike down the ramp, her mother, standing in the crowd, wiped her eyes.

Matt nudged Lennox with his sore elbow. "You should've kept going after I fell, Lennox. You would've had her beat for sure."

"Yeah, maybe. I mean — probably." Lennox nodded.

"Just maybe? Probably?"

"Yeah, sure I would've beat her. But you

needed me, right, Matt?"

David said, "Lennox, I could have helped him, too, you know. If you hadn't already been there."

"You saw me fall, too?" Matt said. "But you didn't stop?"

David said, "Lennox was already there. You didn't need both of us."

The voice on stage babbled on. Matt wasn't listening. He had figured out why Lennox was being so wishy-washy about whether or not he would have won the race. "You *knew* Amanda had you beat when you stopped! Didn't you? You only stopped so you wouldn't look bad losing to a girl!"

Matt felt someone tugging on the sleeve of his T-shirt. It was Mr. Grubb. He was saying, "I wouldn't even have entered my bicycle in the parade if it weren't for you. Come with me."

"What? Where?"

The librarian was still gushing into the microphone.

Mr. Grubb chuckled. "Didn't you hear? We won top prize in the Grand Parade! For the oldest bicycle in the best condition."

By the time they reached the stage, Matt was practically tripping over his feet. Fortunately, he didn't have to speak, because Mr. Grubb was doing plenty of talking. He told the story of when he first got the bike, and the girl he named it after. He described places he'd enjoyed riding it. He told everyone how many years the bike had spent in the attic — "until my new friend, Matt Randall, convinced me to enter it in the parade."

The librarian grabbed her chance to interrupt Mr. Grubb's long speech. "Isn't it wonderful that Pebble Creek's newest resident and its oldest resident have both been honoured with prizes on our centennial?"

The crowd erupted in thunderous applause.

Mr. Grubb turned to Matt. "Would you be so kind as to do the honours?"

Matt gripped the firm handles of the Night-Rider bicycle. He was a little embarrassed, but proud, too, to be called Mr. Grubb's "new friend" in front of the whole town. His head held high, he imagined for a brief moment how it would feel to own this gorgeous bicycle with its cantilever brakes and knobby tires. But, as he wheeled Mr. Grubb's prize down the ramp, he realized that his disappointment at having lost the race had been pushed away. His feelings of admiration for the old man beside him had pushed them away.

When they reached the bottom of the ramp, Mr. Grubb said, "I hate to trouble you, Matt, but would you mind getting that newfangled contraption back to Booth Street for me?"

"Would I mind?!" Matt could already imagine the bike's gears shifting smoothly as he rode through the ravine, the wind cooling his face. His feet almost twitched with eagerness for the new bike's pedals.

"And ..." Mr. Grubb furrowed his bushy brow. "I don't believe there is a lot of room at my place to store it. Do you think there might be somewhere at your house ...?" His voice petered out to nothing, but a boyish twinkle shone in his eyes.

Matt hardly dared believe what it seemed Mr.

Grubb was saying. Get the bike home? Find somewhere to keep it? If Mr. Grubb meant this fabulous mountain bike was a gift, how would he ever thank him?

As if he had read Matt's mind, the old man said, "You've done more for me already than you'll ever know, my friend." Then he rubbed his jowly face and his almost-soft expression toughened. "But don't think you're finished. There is still a huge attic at my house that needs a great deal of sorting and cleaning."

"And ...!" Matt beamed. "I am the guy who can do it!"

"By the way ..." Mr. Grubb turned to go. "Stop in at the library later to see what Amanda did with my baseball card collection. That girl is one smart cookie."

Matt and his friends watched as Mr. Grubb inched his way through the thinning crowd, his body stooped over his old bicycle. The clamour around the stage was fading. The displays and banners were coming down. A short, grey-haired woman called out, "Archie?" Mr. Grubb squinted in the direction of the woman's voice. His mouth dropped open, and slowly he started making his way toward her.

"Hey, Matt," David said, "how about we go for an ice cream? Flavour number six, is it? To celebrate?"

Lennox said, "Can I come too, Matt? Or are you still mad at me about why I really stopped?"

"I'm not mad. At least you stopped. And I'm still not so sure you wouldn't have won that race in the end."

Matt didn't say so, but he was also so happy that Lennox and David were willing to go for ice cream together, he could have forgiven either one of them anything.

The three boys started for the corner.

"Wait a sec," Matt said. "There's someone else who might like to come."

He wheeled over to Amanda and tapped her on the arm. But suddenly he felt awkward about how to invite her. He turned to Amanda's mom. "Would

Amanda like to come with us for ice cream?"

"Why don't you ask her?"

Matt hesitated, then made himself forget about all the people around who might stare. He faked the eating of an ice cream cone, and gestured to Amanda to come along with him and his friends. He heard Lennox titter behind him, but David must have elbowed him in the ribs or something, because he stopped pretty suddenly.

Amanda waved goodbye to her mom, and together she, Matt, David, and Lennox rode away from the crowds.

Amanda looked at the bike Matt was riding, and with her face said, "Like, wow!"

Looking at Amanda's new bike, Matt made his face say the same thing.

Lennox looked at David and shook his head. David just shrugged.

Matt parked his treasured new bike in the rack outside the ice cream store and followed his friends inside. He would have liked to tell Martha all about the race and the parade, but she wasn't working at the ice cream store that day.

Lennox said, "I'm going to try Merry Cherry Berry. No, maybe Grape Bubblegum Delight."

Matt said, "In honour of Mr. Grubb's old-fashioned prize bicycle, I might just go for good, old-fashioned Vanilla."

David said, "I think for me this is the right time for that Mocha Supreme Almond Fudge. But should I have it in a waffle cone, sugar cone, or basket?"

Matt realized suddenly that he should be helping Amanda tell the server what kind of ice cream cone she wanted. After all, he had suggested she come along. He should take some responsibility for her.

He turned to ask what Amanda wanted so he could order it for her. He found her standing in the corner — taking a huge bite out of a giant scoop of Champion Chocolate ice cream on a waffle cone.

She looked at Matt as if to say, "Why are you so surprised?"

After their ice cream, the four kids cycled along the path at the top of the quarry.

"Let's ride to the schoolyard," suggested David.

Lennox started to speed up. "Last one there buys tomorrow's ice cream!"

Lennox and David sped off. Matt was about to holler, "No fair, Amanda couldn't hear what you said." But it seemed Amanda had somehow got the gist of what Lennox had said. And at the rate she was barrelling along, she'd pass both David and Lennox before they even got to the wooden bridge.

Matt let himself fall behind. He'd had enough of tearing around for a while. He wanted instead just to enjoy the softness of the Night-Rider's cushioned seat and the tightness of its chain as he shifted gears.

Things seemed to be working out now, being friends with both Lennox and David. Would Amanda become a friend, too, in time? A girl, and a deaf one at that?

Who knew? Stranger things had happened!

Read more of Matt's adventures in Pebble Creek!

Seven Clues

Matt is so bored. It's summer vacation, all his friends are away, and there is nothing to do in Pebble Creek - that is, until he receives a mysterious postcard.

There's something you should look for.
It will bring you great pleasure
Not coins in a pirate's chest
but a different sort of treasure

A treasure? In Pebble Creek? If Matt had something better to do, he'd throw the postcard away. But he doesn't, and one clue leads to another...

Seven Clues is the first book in Kathy Stinson's trilogy of adventure stories set in Pebble Creek. Enjoy it with *The Great Bike Race* and *One More Clue*-or each story on its own!

ISBN10 1-55028-889-X
ISBN13 978-1-55028-889-6 $8.95

Read more of Matt's adventures in Pebble Creek!

One More Clue

While cleaning his neighbour's attic, Matt uncovers two
mysterious items: a magician's costume and a poem
written on a dusty, yellowed piece of paper.

There's something you should look for
Which I hope that you will treasure
Searching for it by yourself
Is important beyond measure

Could it be an ancient clue for some long-ago treasure hunt? With the help of his friends, Matt sets out to
discover the history of this decades-old mystery-and
possibly a treasure!

One More Clue is the third book in Kathy Stinson's
trilogy of adventure stories set in Pebble Creek. Enjoy it
with *Seven Clues* and *The Great Bike Race*-or each
story on its own!

ISBN10 1-55028-890-3
ISBN13 978-1 55028-890-2 $8.95